The Tortoise and the Hare and *The Lion and the Mouse*

are two fables that readers have loved for generations—and they're both here in this book. When you turn this page, you'll start with *The Tortoise and the Hare*. You'll be able to spot the purple shell of the tortoise and the golden fur of the hare as the rivals get ready for their famous race. Throughout the fable brightly colored shapes appear; use your imagination to turn them into heads and tails, hills, and finish lines.

When you're done, turn the book upside down and start again from the back. This way through, you get the story of *The Lion and the Mouse*. Now watch as the shapes in the art take on a whole new meaning!

In these stories the readers themselves get the chance to decide how the pictures tell the tale. And if two fables aren't enough, why not start the book again and make up your own story to go with the pictures?

There's no limit to the fun you can have. So sit back, open your eyes, and let the fables begin.

To alternative viewpoints
B.O. and S.M.

Published by Dial Books for Young Readers
A Division of Penguin Books USA Inc.
375 Hudson Street, New York, New York 10014

Copyright © 1990 by Suse MacDonald and Bill Oakes
Designed by the authors and Amelia Lau Carling
Printed in Hong Kong by
South China Printing Company (1988) Limited
E
First Edition
1 3 5 7 9 10 8 6 4 2

Library of Congress Cataloging in Publication Data
MacDonald, Suse.
Once upon another / by Suse MacDonald and Bill Oakes.
p.   cm.
Contents: The tortoise and the hare—The lion and the mouse.
ISBN 0-8037-0785-1.—ISBN 0-8037-0787-8 (lib. bdg.)
1. Fables. [1. Fables.] I. Oakes, Bill. II. Title.
PZ8.2.M17On 1990   398.24'52—dc20   [E]   89-23478   CIP   AC

The full-color artwork was created by cutting shapes from
hand-colored rice paper and plain colored-paper and applying
them to a plain background. It was then color-separated and
reproduced as red, blue, yellow, and black halftones.

ONCE UPON ANOTHER

THE TORTOISE AND THE HARE

RETOLD AND ILLUSTRATED BY

Suse MacDonald and Bill Oakes

Dial Books for Young Readers *New York*

"I laughed when you said you would repay me. Now I see that even a lion can use help from a mouse. Thank you," he said as he bowed deeply.

And they were the best of friends from that day forward.

Once upon a time a boastful hare shared a green field with a humble, purple tortoise.

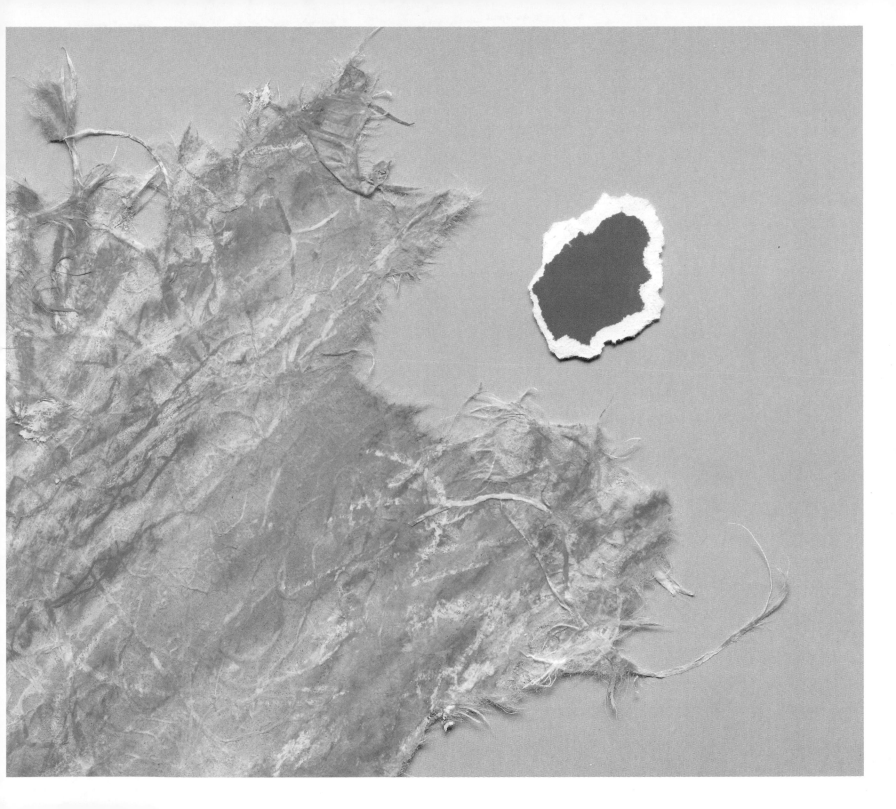

When they arrived, the lion gently put the mouse down among a crowd of admiring friends.

In front of the tortoise's friends the golden hare would often say, "You're so slow you would lose a race with the grass."

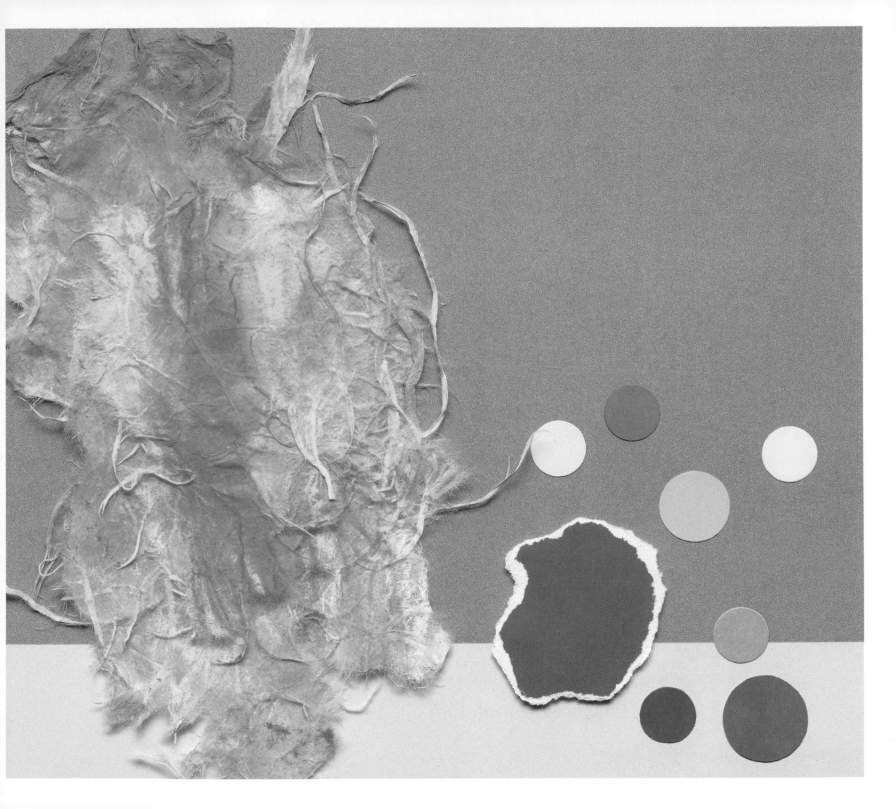

The lion knelt down so the mouse could scamper to the top of his hairy crown. There the mouse sat happily as the lion walked proudly toward the meadow.

Then the hare would race around the meadow showing off, almost knocking the tortoise over. The tortoise watched patiently. He was so slow it even took him a long time to get angry.

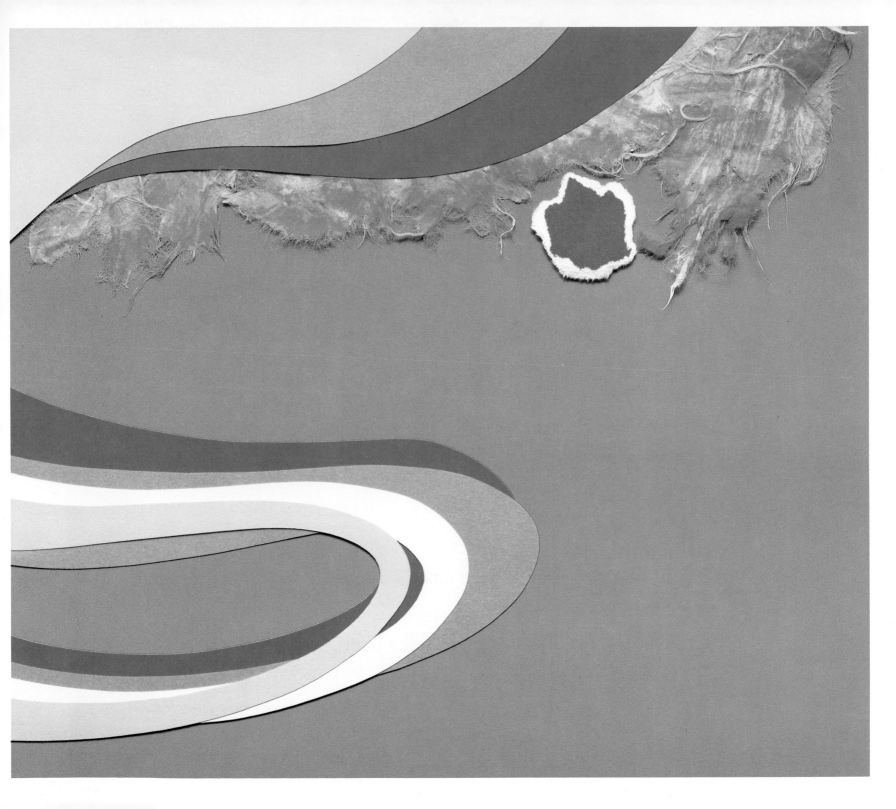

Gathering all his courage, the mouse ran up one of the great ropes that bound the lion and gnawed it until it parted.

"You've saved my life," said the grateful lion. "Now what may I do for you?"

"We-l-l-l-l," said the mouse, and he whispered in the lion's ear.

But one day the tortoise snapped back, "You may be fast, but I can be first."

"Oh, ho, ho, the slowpoke talks back," teased the hare. "Don't you know? Fast is always first."

"We'll just see," said the tortoise. "How about a race?"

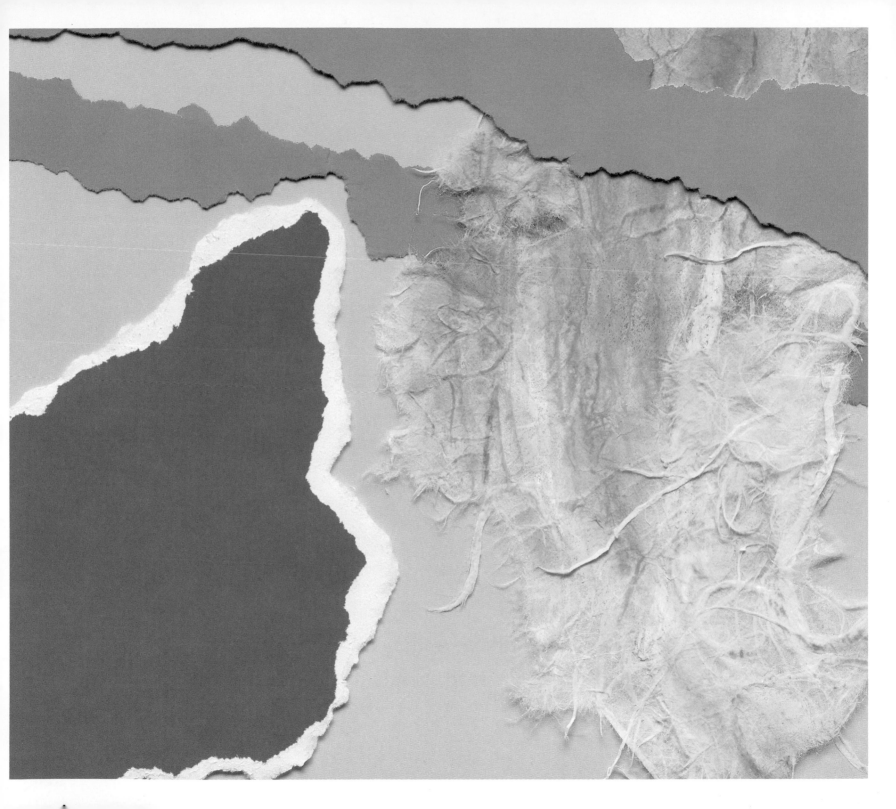

The hare leaped up. "What a great idea! First one to the old mill wins." And without waiting for the tortoise to reply, he dashed off down the road. Slowly the tortoise set off after him.

When he entered the forest, he saw the lion caught in the net with only his large nose sticking out.

The hare ran until he reached a pond with sticks floating on the surface. Soon he was so busy gazing at his reflection that he didn't notice the tortoise pass by.

"No matter," he said when he finally looked up, "I'll be ahead of him in a flash."

Nearly beaten, he only had strength for one last roar. And roar he did until the forest rumbled with the noise. Nearby the mouse heard him. Why, it's the lion. He's in trouble, thought the mouse as he hurried off toward the commotion.

And sure enough, he whooshed past the tortoise a second time. Before long he was so far in front that the tortoise was only a speck on the horizon.

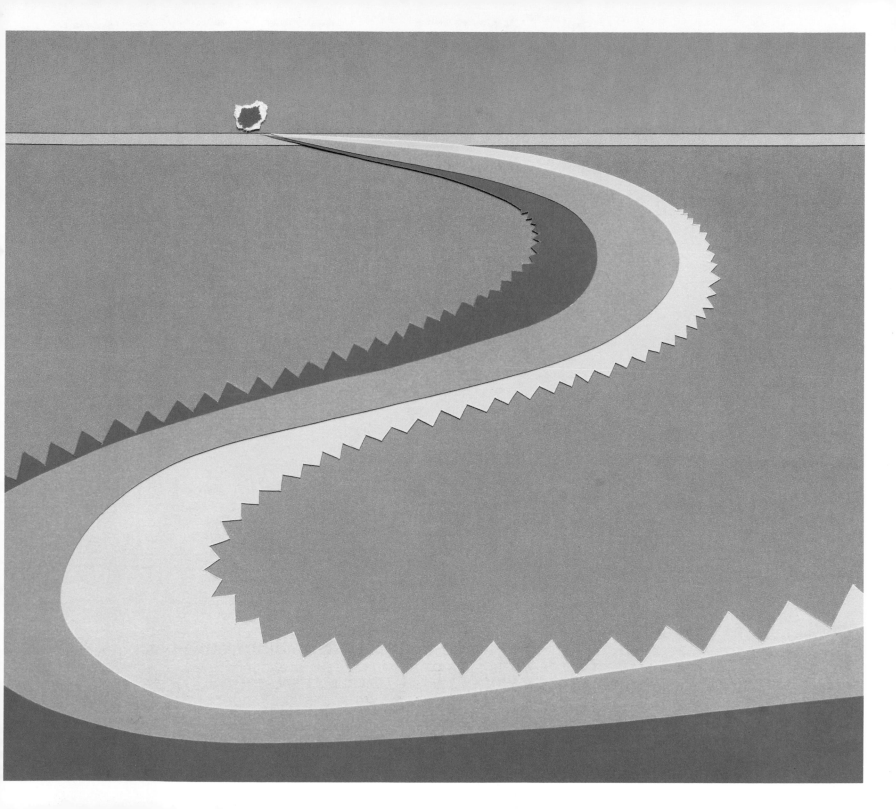

All night the lion struggled to free himself. He kicked, thrashed, and chewed on the ropes that bound him, but he could not escape. By morning he was very tired and so tangled he could not move at all.

Soon there was nothing on the road but a comfortable bush just right for a nap. I've got plenty of time, thought the overconfident hare. And he fell asleep in the sunny branches.

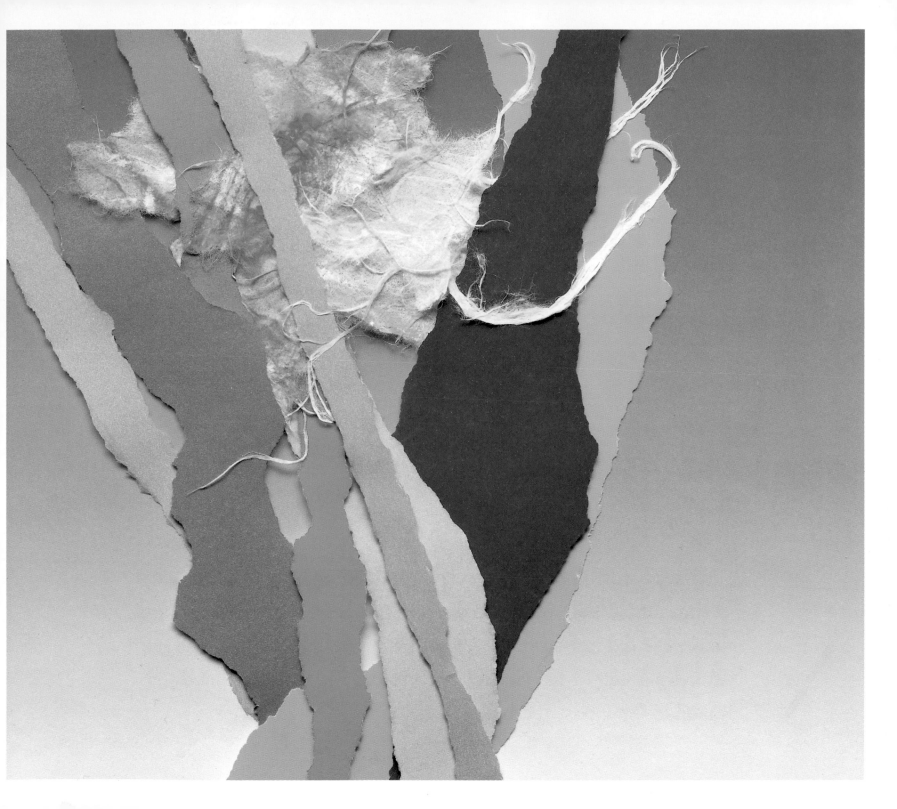

Later, when the mouse was safe in his nest, the lion went looking for dinner. He saw the glow of many eyes peering at him from the deep dark forest. As he went into the trees, he was so busy thinking about his meal, he got careless and walked right into a hunter's net.

Meanwhile the weary tortoise plodded on, one slow step at a time. It was late in the morning when he reached the sleeping hare. He did not stop. He did not even hesitate. While the hare was dreaming of his victory celebration, the tortoise quietly made his way past the bush.

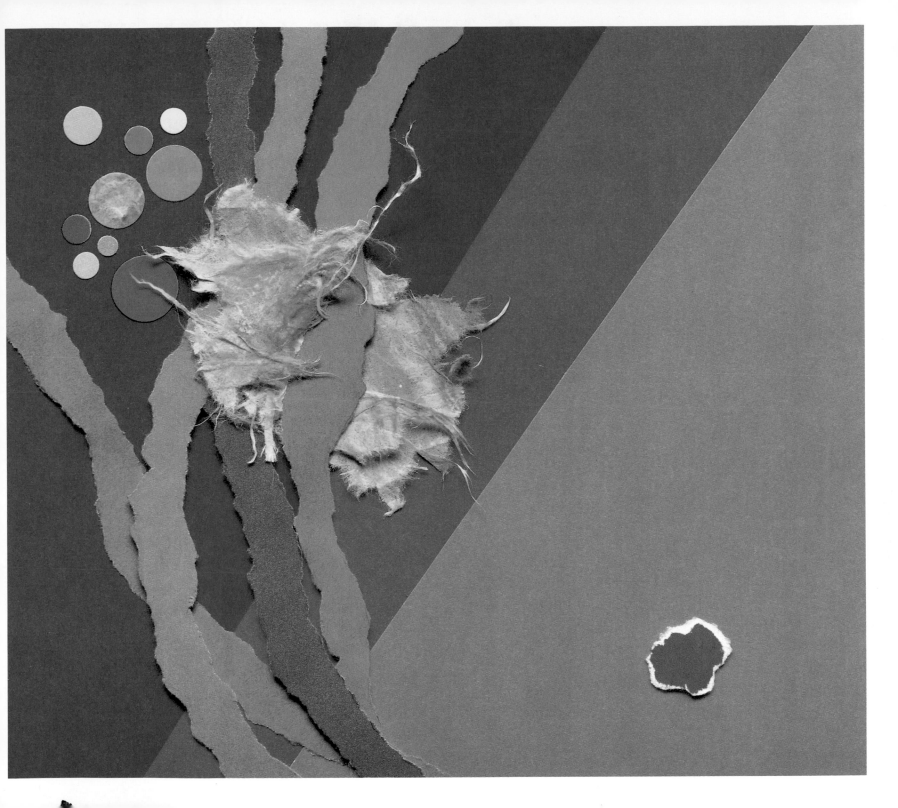

"Then you'll make a tasty snack," said the lion.

"But wait," said the mouse, "who knows when you might need help from someone my size?"

The lion was amused, and after a moment he let the mouse scamper back to his friends.

For the rest of that long, long day, the tortoise bobbled along. As he arrived at the finish line, the cheers of the crowd woke the sleeping hare. That tortoise can't beat me, he thought. Bounding to his feet, the hare dashed off.

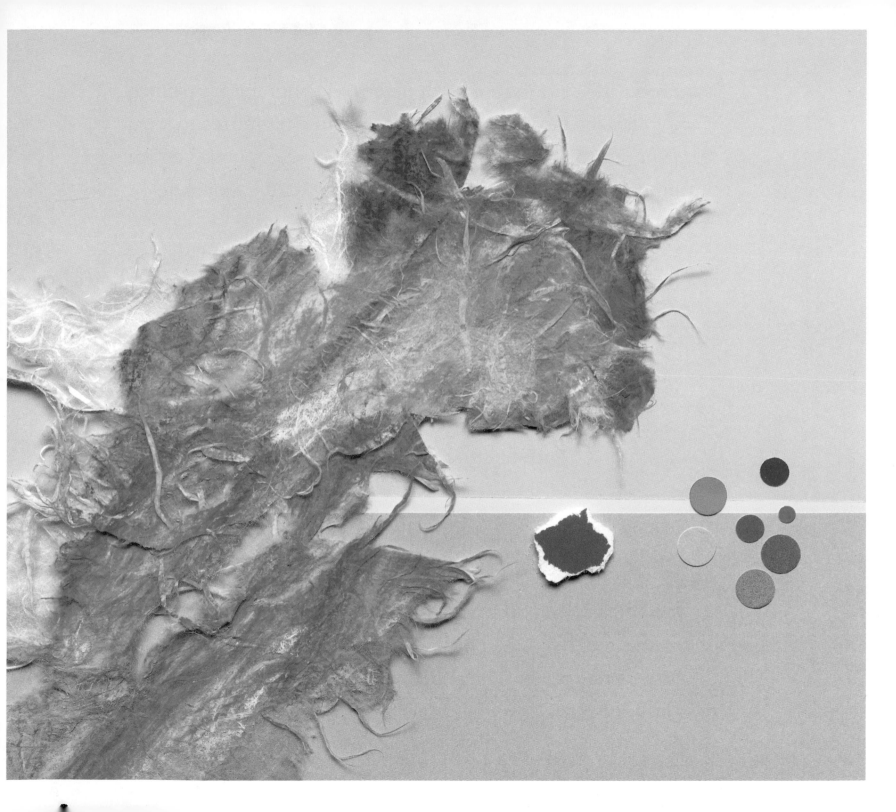

Suddenly a great hairy paw reached out and held him fast to the ground. The frightened mouse struggled to get his little head out from underneath. "Oh spare me, your majesty," he begged. "I am much too small to be a meal for your nobleness."

The tortoise was so tired he was tempted to stop for a rest only a few feet from the finish. But then the long shadow of the hare's body fell on him. He knew he had to keep going or he'd lose the race.

Without looking back, he crept into the long grass and tiptoed toward the sleeping beast.

When the exhausted tortoise finally stepped across the line, he was only a second ahead of the astonished hare.

When he told his friends, they cried, "Oh don't! The lion will wake up and eat you."

"Oh, pooh," said the mouse. "The lion is fast asleep. I am so light he will never know I'm there. Just think of the fun I'll have seeing the world from the top of his head."

The cheering crowd gathered around the happy tortoise. The hare sheepishly shook the dust from his coat.

"Well," he said, "I guess being fast isn't the only thing you need to be first. I'll never tease you again."

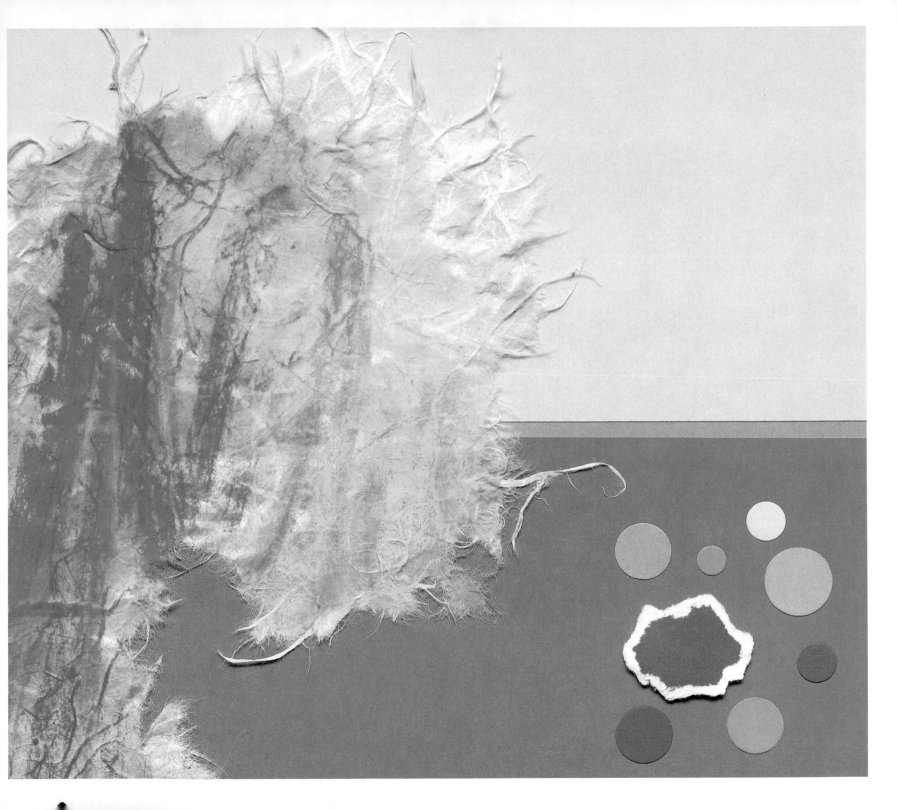

A lion lay asleep in a clearing, resting his golden head on his paws. His long tail stretched out behind him. Nearby lived an adventurous purple mouse who was thinking what fun it would be to hide himself in the lion's mane.

"Good," said the tortoise, and together they walked slowly back to their meadow.

ONCE UPON ANOTHER

THE LION AND THE MOUSE

RETOLD AND ILLUSTRATED BY

Suse MacDonald and Bill Oakes

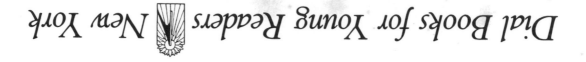

Dial Books for Young Readers ◆ New York